# QUORK ATTACK

**Alison Hawes**
**Illustrated by Stephen Player**

RIGBY

# Chapter 1

Nick and Jonathan loved playing computer games.

"That's the one I want!" said Jonathan, pointing to the computer game in the shop window.

"*Quork Attack,*" said Nick, reading the box. "I've heard that's great!"

"Come on," said Jonathan. "Let's go in and buy it!"

The shop was full of games, but *Quork Attack* definitely looked the most exciting. The boys hurried back to Jonathan's house with the game, eager to try it out.

As soon as they got back, they raced up to Jonathan's bedroom. While Jonathan loaded the game, Nick took a long look at the box.

The box was covered with pictures of blue and red creatures, zapping each other. The Pods were bright blue, potato-shaped creatures with powerful slime-rays. Their enemies, the Quorks, were small, red creatures with ten long spikes for legs. They looked really nasty.

 • "OK, I've loaded it," said Jonathan.
"Are you ready to play?"

   "Let's go!" said Nick, taking a seat next to
him at the computer. Nick felt a tingling
thrill at the back of his neck, as he always
did when he was about to play a new game.
You never knew quite what to expect!

The boys played all afternoon, helping the Pods defend their planet from the horrible Quorks. They found it much harder than they thought it would be. No matter what they did, the Pods were being wiped out very quickly.

"I don't understand it!" said Jonathan in despair. "Nothing we do seems to make any difference."

"I know," said Nick. "Usually we get better at these games, not worse!"

Jonathan tried so hard to help the Pods that he began to really hate the Quorks. Then he started to have strange feelings about the Pods – it was as if they were too sad and weak to help themselves.

"This might sound weird," said Jonathan, "but it's almost like the Pods don't want to fight!"

"Don't be silly, Jonathan," said Nick. "It's only a game. No one gets hurt. It's not real. Quorks and Pods don't have feelings!"

"I said it would sound weird!" said Jonathan.

"Oh, I give up," said Nick, half an hour later. "I think there's something wrong with this game!"

"Come on," said Jonathan. "Let's get a drink, and then we'll play one more game."

"OK, just one more game and then I'm going home."

At first, when the boys went back upstairs, everything looked the same. Then they looked at the computer screen, and they could see something was very wrong. There were Quorks everywhere, hundreds of them, but not a single Pod could be seen!

Not one!

"Where are all the Pods?" asked Jonathan, clicking the computer mouse. "We can't have lost them all! Where can they be?"

"Maybe they've escaped!" joked Nick.

Nick looked at Jonathan and saw he wasn't laughing. "What's the matter?" Nick said, frowning. "It was only a joke!"

"Look!" said Jonathan, pointing to the floor.

"Where?" said Nick.

"There on the floor!" Jonathan whispered.

Nick looked down. "They look exactly like tiny slime-rays," he said with a gasp.

"Exactly," whispered Jonathan. "It's not a joke, Nick. The Pods really *have* escaped, and they've dropped their slime-rays."

"What do we do now?" asked Nick.
He was beginning to feel frightened.

"I don't know," said Jonathan, "but I *do*
know we have to find those Pods."

Nick and Jonathan searched the room
frantically, but they didn't find a single Pod.

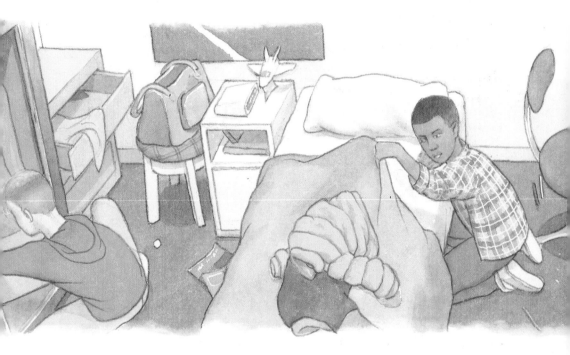

After a while, it was time for Nick to go
home. Jonathan felt totally confused.

"I think I'll stop looking," he said.

Maybe they'd just played too many
computer games.

# Chapter 2

Jonathan woke up suddenly in the middle of the night. At first he didn't know what had woken him. Then he heard something.
It was a small, muffled, bleeping sound, like someone crying into a pillow.

Jonathan looked around in the dark, trying to find where the noise was coming from. That was when he saw the light. A bright blue light was coming from the front pocket of his school bag.

Quietly, Jonathan got out of bed, tiptoed over to the bag, and peered into the pocket. There were all the Pods, huddled together, and bleeping softly.

"It's OK," Jonathan whispered. "I'm not going to hurt you!"

The bleeping suddenly stopped, as if the Pods understood.

"You'll be safe with me," said Jonathan, quickly zipping up the pocket so they couldn't escape again.

"I'll decide what to do with you in the morning, when Nick comes before school."

Jonathan could hardly sleep for the rest of the night.

The next morning, Jonathan showed Nick where the Pods were hiding.

"They look very pale," said Nick, as he peered into the pocket. "I thought the Pods were bright blue."

"That's odd," said Jonathan. "They were bright blue last night. Do you think they might be sick?"

Nick put his hand into the pocket and scooped out some of the Pods. He looked at them, pale and weak in his hand.

"I think it's worse than that," said Nick. "I think they're dying!"

"Maybe they can't survive for long outside a computer," said Nick.

"I think you're right," said Jonathan as he loaded the game again. "The sooner we get them back on here, the better!"

"No," said Nick, "We can't! They haven't got their slime-rays. They won't survive without them!"

"I thought you were the one who said they weren't real. You said it was just a game," said Jonathan. "Now I don't know what to do," he said in despair. "If we put them back, they'll die. If we *don't* put them back, they'll die!"

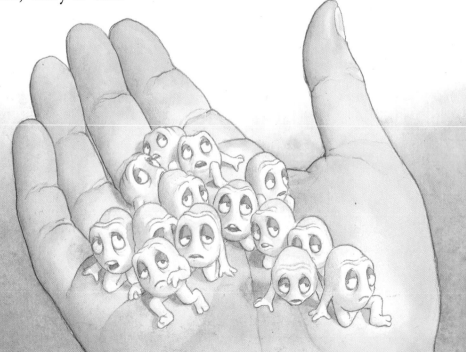

Nick wasn't listening. He was pointing at the computer screen.

"Look!" he said, with a gasp.

Jonathan spun around to see what was happening. The Quorks had stopped running around and were all huddled together in one corner of the screen.

"What are they doing?" asked Nick.

"I don't know," said Jonathan.

Then suddenly, the tip of one long, thin, red leg started to come through the screen.

"Oh, no! Quick!" yelled Nick.

Just in time, Jonathan clicked on the mouse and closed the game.

"Now what do we do?" he said, taking out the CD.

Nick thought hard. "What we need is a blank disk to put the Pods on," he said at last.

"Great idea," said Jonathan, "but we'll have to be quick. I don't think there's much time left!"

They both looked at the Pods, who by now were almost white. They were bleeping very quietly.

"Quick!" said Nick, as Jonathan put a blank disk into the computer.

"Ready," said Jonathan.

Nick held the Pods up to the screen and one by one they jumped back through it.

The screen flashed twice and then lots of bright blue Pods appeared. They were grinning and bleeping happily. Nick and Jonathan jumped for joy.

"We did it! We saved them!" shouted Nick.

Then the screen went blank for a second and a message appeared.

**THANK YOU . . .**
**WE ARE ENJOYING**
**THE PEACE AND**
**QUIET AT LAST**

"So are we!" Nick and Jonathan said together.

"The only place this is going now is in the bin!" said Jonathan, throwing away the game.

"Absolutely!" said Nick with a grin.